Authorized Walt Disney Productions' Edition

THE RESCUERS

Featuring characters from the Disney film suggested by the books by Margery Sharp,
"The Rescuers" and "Miss Bianca," published by Little, Brown & Company

gb **GOLDEN PRESS • NEW YORK**

Western Publishing Company, Inc.
Racine, Wisconsin

Bernard was a typical little mouse. He had bright eyes and a turned up nose and a fine, long tail. There was nothing very special about Bernard. In any crowd of mice, he was just another mouse. But Bernard was very proud to be part of the International Rescue Aid Society—that organization of brave and noble mice who help people in trouble.

Yes, Bernard was very proud of the Society, even if he wasn't really a member. He was actually the janitor, but he was the janitor at the International Headquarters in the basement of the United Nations Building in New York City.

One day the chairman of the Society called Bernard into his office. The chairman was a very important and wise mouse with graying whiskers, and when he spoke everyone paid strict attention. "Bernard," the chairman said, "I have called an emergency meeting of the Rescue Aid Society! You must have everything ready when the delegates arrive." The chairman smiled a kindly smile. "I'm sure I can count on you," he told Bernard. "You are as loyal and hardworking as any member of our group, even if you aren't really a member!"

Bernard absolutely glowed with pleasure when the chairman said this, and he ran off and immediately set to work cleaning up the Assembly Hall where the delegates would gather. The Assembly Hall was really a forgotten storage room in the basement of the great United Nations Building.

Soon the delegates began to arrive. Although they were each and every one of them mice, they looked quite a bit like delegates to the United Nations itself. Some wore the dark suits and tall hats of professional diplomats. Others were dressed in their native costumes. Bernard was very impressed as they all took their places. The chairman rapped with his gavel and waited for them to be quiet, and then began to explain why he had called this special meeting.

But then, "Miss Bianca!" someone cried. "Here comes Miss Bianca!" And Bianca hurried into the room, smiling and waving to her friends. Bernard's heart gave a thump, for he was sure she was the most beautiful mouse in the world. She had lovely big eyes and tiny paws. She was always dressed in the latest styles, and she wore the most enchanting perfume. "Hello, everyone!" she cried. "Oh, I'm so sorry to be late!"

"You're always late," the chairman said, but he smiled when he said it and he waited until Bianca had found a seat among the delegates in the front row. Then he went on with his speech. "I have reason to believe that someone is in trouble and needs our help!" he announced solemnly. He motioned to Bernard, who was waiting near a long curtain which hung in a corner of the room. Bernard quickly pulled a cord and the curtain opened. Behind it was a dirt-stained bottle. Plainly it was a very important bottle, for there was a note inside.

"Two of our agents found this bottle floating in the harbor and brought it to us!" announced the chairman. Then he signaled again to Bernard, who knew exactly what to do. He threw a coil of rope over one shoulder and pushed a mouse-sized stepladder against the side of the bottle. When he had climbed to the top of the ladder, he was only at the base of the bottle's neck. Undaunted, he made a lasso with the rope, and with the skill of an old-time cowboy he looped the rope over the cork at the top of the bottle.

"My goodness!" Bianca exclaimed. "How clever he is!" Bernard pretended not to hear her. He went on with his job. He clambered up the rope to the lip of the bottle, wrapping both arms around the cork. He twisted and grunted and tugged, and at last the cork popped out. Some of the delegates called to him to be careful and some were sure he was going to fall, but he didn't. He tipped and swayed on the lip of the bottle, but he kept his balance and gave them a brave smile.

Actually, Bernard didn't feel very brave, but he was determined to do his job for the Rescue Aid Society. He dropped the rope from the lip of the bottle down to the inside, squeezed himself through the neck, slid down the rope, and seized the piece of paper. He then heaved the note up through the mouth

of the bottle, and all the mice waiting below crowded around to catch the note and read it.

It was faded and crumpled and parts of it were water-stained, but the chairman could clearly see that the message was addressed to the Morningside Orphanage in New York. "It appears to have been written by a child," said the chairman. "It says, 'I am in terrible trouble and . . .'" The chairman could make out no more of the note except for the sentence at the end: "Please help me!" It was signed, "Penny."

"Penny!" Bianca murmured. "A little girl! A poor lost orphan, perhaps!" Miss Bianca looked very determined. "Mr. Chairman, we must do something to help this child! I know we haven't much to go on, but we must try." Bianca then gave the chairman her most winning smile. "Please," she said, "may I have this assignment?"

"You?" said the chairman. He was greatly surprised. "A lady? It's—it's highly irregular!" He frowned for a moment. Then he shrugged his little mouse shoulders and decided that there was nothing in the bylaws of the International Rescue Aid Society that would prevent a lady from trying to help an orphan.

Bernard had been clinging to the top of the bottle, listening and watching. He knew that Bianca was clever and courageous, but he also thought she was delicate and dainty. "Mr. Chairman!" he shouted suddenly. "I think Miss Bianca should have a co-agent go with her. This assignment may be dangerous."

The chairman grumbled and snorted. He glared at the little janitor and he reminded Bernard that he *was* a janitor and that he was interrupting an important meeting. But he knew Bernard was right. "All right, ladies and gentlemen," he said finally. "*I* have decided that a co-agent shall go with Miss Bianca. Who will volunteer?"

There wasn't a delegate in the room who wouldn't have given his whiskers to accompany Bianca, and there wasn't a delegate in the room who didn't put up his hand. Bianca was pleased, of course. What lady wouldn't be pleased at such a show of gallantry? "I thank you all for volunteering," she told them. "It is a most difficult decision." She thought for a moment, and then she pointed to Bernard. "I choose Mr. Bernard!"

Standing on the top of the bottle, Bernard blinked and gulped with surprise. Then he lost his balance. He slid down the side of the bottle and caught onto the ladder just in time. He climbed down to the ground and he stared at Bianca, embarrassed. "But . . . but . . ." he stammered. "I'm only a janitor."

"No matter," said Bianca cheerfully. "We'll make a fine team, Mr. Bernard! Now we mustn't waste a moment. We can guess that Penny is a little girl who needs help, and we know that she tried to send a note to the Morningside Orphanage. We will look up the address of the orphanage in the telephone book, and we will start our search there!"

◆·◆·◆·◆·◆·◆·◆

Night had fallen over New York City when Bernard and Bianca left the United Nations Building, and it had started to rain. They scampered down one shadowed street and up the next. The headlights of passing automobiles almost blinded them. To get out of the rain, they stopped under a mailbox to look at a city map. "Here it is," Bernard said, "three blocks down and four blocks over." With determination they trudged on and at last came to a large, pleasant-looking building with the sign "Morningside Orphanage" over the front door. No light showed anywhere in the place, but this did not dismay the mice. A clever mouse can operate most efficiently in the dark. Bernard located an open window, and he and Bianca scrambled up onto the window ledge and peered inside.

"This must be the dormitory," Bianca murmured as she viewed a huge room lined with beds which were spaced several feet from one another. A small child slept in each one. "How sad! Look at those poor darlings with no mothers or fathers!"

Bernard agreed that it was indeed sad, but after musing on this for only a moment he hopped down to the floor to begin the search for a clue to the whereabouts of the child named Penny. Bianca jumped down after him, and the two mice began to explore the dormitory. There was a name plate at the foot of each bed, and the mice checked each of these. There was none for Penny. Then Bernard noticed a small cardboard carton in a storage closet. "*Penny's things,*" he whispered, reading the hand-printed sign on the box. "*Hold until further notice.*"

Without hesitating, the two mice clambered into the carton and began searching among the things that were stowed there. They found a doll and a pair of old tennis shoes. They found some hair ribbons and some crayons and some books. Then they heard a scratching sound at the open top of the box and found that they were staring straight into the face of a large, gray-whiskered cat.

"Mice!" exclaimed the cat. "Oh, my! Why couldn't you have found some other place to hide?" The cat sat down and yawned a weary yawn. "I hope you don't plan on living here," he said. "I'm supposed to chase mice out of the orphanage, but I'm getting too old for that. If anyone found out, I'd lose my job!"

Bianca had trembled at the first sight of the cat, but now she took heart and explained that she and Bernard were looking for a little girl named Penny. That seemed to change things completely so far as the cat was concerned. "Any friends of Penny's are friends of mine!" he declared. "She's my favorite orphan. We used to talk together all the time. By the way, my name is Rufus."

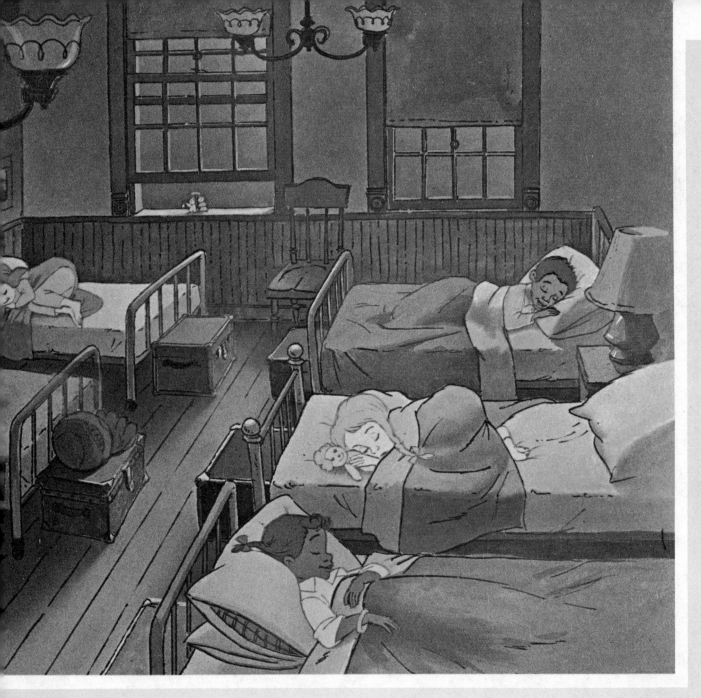

The mice climbed out of the carton and introduced themselves, and of course Bernard asked, "Where is Penny, Rufus?"

"I don't know," the cat answered sadly. "The folks here think she ran away, but I'm not sure. I know she was unhappy because she hadn't been adopted, but all the other children liked her. Of course, she had me to talk to, and Teddy, her little stuffed bear. She took Teddy with her wherever she went." Rufus then went on to tell the mice about the day Penny disappeared. "She and Teddy were out in front of the orphanage when that lady came along and tried to give her a ride in her automobile. I don't like that lady, so I didn't hang around, but I'm sure Penny wouldn't go anywhere with her. She and her partner run a sleazy pawnshop down the street."

"But she might have been the last one to see Penny here at the orphanage!" Bernard exclaimed. "That may be a clue! Miss Bianca, we'd better investigate that pawnshop!" With that, Bernard thanked Rufus for his help, and he and Bianca hurried through the dormitory and slipped out of the window without waking any of the sleeping children. They ran down the deserted street and found the pawnshop which Rufus the cat had described.

The store was dingy and dilapidated, and the nervous mice crept into it through a space at the bottom of the door. Faint night lights cast weird shadows on the array of dusty items that lined the counters and shelves. "Whoever owns this shop is a terrible housekeeper!" Bianca observed.

But Bernard wasn't listening. Bernard had spied a small book which someone had tossed carelessly in a corner. Together he and Bianca opened the cover. Penny's name was written in crayon inside the book. "So Penny *has* been here!" Bianca declared. "Could she still be here? We must search and . . ."

Before she could finish what she was saying, there was a whirring sound followed by a rasp, and a cuckoo popped out of an old clock to announce the hour. Both mice froze with alarm. Then Bianca giggled and pointed to Bernard's tail. "Look! Your tail! It's all frizzy! I do believe that clock frightened you!" Then, because she was truly a kind and gentle mouse, Bianca stopped giggling. Instead she smiled and decided that Bernard was not so much frightened as surprised. She smoothed the wiry hairs on Bernard's tail back into place. "I am sure you are very brave, Bernard," she said.

Before Bernard could answer, a telephone on an old-fashioned desk rang loudly. Bernard's tail frizzled again, and both mice scurried to hide in the shadows. An instant later, a door at the back of the store opened and a tall, evil-looking woman stormed in. Her long hair was tangled and unkempt, and her dark eyes flashed with anger. "Who can be calling

called Devil's Bayou! Come on! We've got to go with that woman!"

The two mice scampered after Medusa, and when they reached the back room she was already hurling clothes into a large suitcase. Bernard waited until she had her back turned, then hopped into the open suitcase and hid. But before Bianca could join him, the woman had turned back and slammed the lid shut. Bernard was trapped inside. In her haste,

at this time of night?" she raged, but when she picked up the telephone her voice became sickly sweet. "Madame Medusa's Pawnshop Boutique," she said. "Madame Medusa speaking. May I help you?"

Bernard and Bianca had no doubt that this person named Madame Medusa was the unpleasant woman Rufus had told them about. They heard her say, "Mr. Snoops! Don't tell me. Let me guess! You've found the diamond!" She paused for a moment, and then she exploded in a new and sudden fury. "You fool! You should have made Penny get the diamond for us by now! And . . . and she what? She's been sending messages for help in bottles? You idiot, Snoops! Can't you even control a little girl? I'm taking the next plane down to Devil's Bayou, and I'll take care of Penny when I get there!" She slammed the telephone down and started toward the door at the back of the shop.

"Devil's Bayou!" whispered Bernard. "They must be holding Penny prisoner in a place

however, Medusa did not notice that the sleeve of a dress hung out of the case. Bianca noticed. Bianca took hold of that sleeve and hung on.

Still grumbling about Mr. Snoops, Madame Medusa carried the suitcase out the back door of the pawnshop. A huge, very old limousine stood in the dark alley, and she tossed the luggage onto the back seat. A moment later, Medusa was behind the steering wheel of the car and speeding through the city streets. The tires screeched as the limousine skidded around corners and careened through stop lights. The engine roared as it raced along the deserted pavement. Then there was a turn that was too sharp. The car lurched sideways and the back door flew open. The suitcase sailed out with Bianca still clinging to it!

Wham! The case hit a telephone pole and popped open. Bianca found herself on the

ground, staring at the broken case and at the tangle of mussed clothes inside. After a second, a small nose appeared from beneath the clothes. Then Bianca saw a pair of bewildered eyes. Finally Bernard stumbled out, groggy and dazed. "Gosh, that was a rough trip!" he exclaimed. "Are we at Devil's Bayou already?"

"No, and I'm afraid we've lost our ride," said Bianca. "But at least we know where Penny is." She tugged at Bernard's sleeve. "Come along! We'll pick up our luggage from headquarters and fly to the bayou!"

A few hours later, the two mice were scampering across the roof of one of New York City's tallest buildings. There was a heliport there, and helicopter flights left for the major airports. Bernard struggled with Bianca's suitcase and with his own, and Bianca carried a bright new umbrella, since she believed in being prepared for anything, including sudden rains. They dashed between the feet of the people who hurried toward the waiting helicopters and continued on toward the far side of the roof, to the small, weather-beaten shack which was the main office of Albatross Airlines. "I certainly hope their planes are in better condition than their office," Bianca murmured as they entered the shabby little building by walking up an old cleated chicken ramp.

The place was deserted. A battered desk stood in one corner and an ancient radio with a huge loudspeaker was opposite the desk. On the back wall was a bulletin board with the flight schedule of this remarkable airline scribbled in chalk. Bernard read the board and he groaned. "Oh, no!" he said. "We're too late! Albatross Flight Thirteen left at 6:45!"

"I'm sure they wouldn't leave without us,"

Bianca assured him, and she patted him on the back. "After all, the chairman of the Society made reservations for us, and we have been quite lucky up until now, haven't we?"

Bernard wasn't terribly sure that a reservation on Flight 13 was lucky, and his tail began to frizzle again, but before he could say anything, a loud squawk came from the radio loudspeaker. "Flight Thirteen to tower, Flight Thirteen to tower!" an irate voice shouted. "Come in, tower! Dag nabit, down there! Where is everybody? I need permission to land! Traffic up here is thicker than . . ." There was a tremendous roar, followed by another angry squawk. "A super-jet just singed my tail feathers!"

Bernard blinked and hurried to pick up the microphone beside the old radio. "Hello, sir," he said nervously. "We . . . uh . . . we just got here, sir, and . . . uh . . . you have *our* permission to land!"

"Well, it's about time!" the voice answered. Bianca ran to the doorway to watch. Overhead, a large albatross circled gracefully, his huge wings rising and falling lazily as he approached the rooftop. He was flying beautifully until his feet touched the runway. Then he seemed to lose control, skidding, sliding, bouncing, skidding again, and he flapped his wings furiously until he braked to a jolting stop. He straightened himself, lifted the old-fashioned goggles from his eyes, and said proudly, "One of my better landings!"

Bernard gasped, but Bianca smiled her most dazzling smile. "Captain," she said. "You certainly fly beautifully."

The albatross, who turned out to be named Orville, was a trifle embarrassed at this, but he was also pleased. He assured the mice that Flight 13 would take off just as soon as he caught his breath. "Climb aboard and make yourselves comfortable," he told them. "Take any of the seats in the first-class section!"

Bianca and Bernard climbed up Orville's

outstretched wing and saw an empty sardine can strapped to his back. Plainly it was the first-class section. It had to be. It was the only section. Bianca climbed into the can with her umbrella, and Bernard squeezed in beside her. Orville checked his wing feathers and his tail. "This is your captain speaking," he called over his shoulder. "Fasten your seat belts, and no smoking. Here we go!"

There was a runway marked on the roof of the building. Orville began to plod along this runway. He went slowly at first, then faster and faster, and he began to flap his mighty wings. Bernard held on for dear life, certain that the big bird would never be able to get into the air. The edge of the roof came closer and closer, and at the very last moment they sailed into space, and Orville's wings carried them aloft. Bernard felt himself trembling, wishing with all his heart that they had taken the train, but Orville was as proud of his take-off as he had been of his wobbling, bouncing landing.

"I understand you folks have tickets through to Devil's Bayou," Orville remarked. He made a slow, graceful turn above New York. The lights in the city below twinkled like many-colored stars. "That bayou's a pretty dismal place. The last time I flew over it, I got caught in a thunderstorm that really shook my pinfeathers!"

"Ohhh!" Bernard moaned. "I don't like thunderstorms when I'm safely on the ground! I certainly don't want to fly into one!"

"You worry too much," Bianca assured him. She leaned over and gave him a little kiss on the cheek. "You must relax, Bernard."

◆·◆·◆·◆·◆·◆·◆

While Bianca slept peacefully and Bernard dozed and woke and vowed that he would be very brave, and then dozed again, Madame Medusa came to her secret hideout in Devil's Bayou. It was an old riverboat which rested on a sandbar in the middle of the swamp. Years before it had been abandoned and left

to rot, but Medusa and Mr. Snoops had found it and had made it their headquarters. It was in the darkness just before dawn that Medusa stalked on board and began to shout. "Penny!" she called. "Penny, where are you?"

There was no answer, and Medusa raged through the old boat, turning on lights and searching every corner. At last Medusa burst out onto the deck, waving her fists. "That little brat has escaped again!" she howled. "Mr. Snoops, you fool! Bring Nero and Brutus!"

A moment later, Snoops came onto the deck. He was a short pudgy man with thick glasses and an oily, nervous smile. He was followed by two vicious-appearing alligators who ambled past him and approached Medusa. "Ohh!" she crooned. "Brutus! Nero! Quickly, go find Penny and bring her back!"

The two huge beasts yawned and showed their sharp teeth. Then they slithered down the gangplank and disappeared into the murky darkness, while Snoops fretted and whined and worried lest they hurt the little girl. "Nero and Brutus know what they're doing," declared Medusa coldly, "and that is more than I can say for you!" Medusa stamped to the side of the boat. "I'm going to take my Swamplaunch and help them!"

The Swamplaunch was Medusa's own invention. Once it had been a simple rowboat, but she had added some special features. There were headlights in the front, and a windshield and a steering wheel and all of the things that are usually found in an automobile. In the back, however, there was a pair of jet engines.

As Snoops watched, Madame Medusa

climbed into the launch, sat down behind the steering wheel, and pressed the starter button. Nothing happened. "The key," Snoops suggested timidly. "I think you forgot to turn the key." Which she had, although she didn't want to admit it. But once the key was turned in the ignition, the engines thundered to life. The headlights glowed. Even the windshield wipers worked. "You fool, Snoops!" Medusa screamed. "Send up the flares. Light up the swamp so I can find Penny!" A blast of flame shot from the jets, and Medusa and her Swamplaunch swept off into the darkness.

Snoops dashed down to the engine room of the riverboat. A large pile of fireworks stood there, next to a rusty old furnace. Snoops opened the furnace, put a skyrocket inside, and aimed the rocket up the smokestack. Then he lit the fuse, slammed the furnace door, and plugged his ears with his fingers.

At this very moment, Orville was flying over Devil's Bayou. Bernard and Bianca, in their seat on his back, watched as he circled slowly down toward the mysterious swamp. "This is your Captain speaking," Orville announced briskly. "Flight Thirteen is now making its final approach and we are preparing to land. The crew and I thank you for flying the happy skies of Albatross Airr . . ur . . ur . . .!"

Wham! A skyrocket exploded nearby. Whizzing balls of sparks whistled through the air, and shooting stars lit the swamp below. Boom! Another rocket zoomed past them and burst into blinding flares. "Orville!" Bernard shouted. "What's going on?"

"Darned if I know!" cried Orville. "Maybe Waldo the Kid has come back to the bayou! He and his gang were pirates and they lived here years ago when . . ." Another skyrocket zipped by, sliced through Orville's tail feathers, and exploded into sparkling lights. "Awkkk! My rudder's been clipped!" squawked Orville. But then he remembered that he was, after all, the pilot of an airliner. "This is your Captain speaking," he shouted. He was bouncing about wildly. "In the event of an emergency, the stewardess will direct you to the proper exits!"

"But there is no stewardess!" Bernard cried.

"Then bail out!" ordered Orville, and he spun in a tight circle to avoid another skyrocket. Bianca bailed out. She was, in fact, tossed out into space. "Bernard!" she cried. "Help! Bernard!"

Bernard didn't stop to think. He seized Bianca's closed umbrella and dove from Orville's back. Down, down he plunged through the darkness until he overtook Bianca. Then he grabbed her with one hand and held the umbrella up with the other. Pop! The umbrella opened like a parachute, and they were floating gently toward the swamp. "Oh, Bernard!" said Bianca. "You *are* so brave!"

◆ · ◆ · ◆ · ◆ · ◆ · ◆ · ◆

A hillbilly swamp rat named Luke sat on

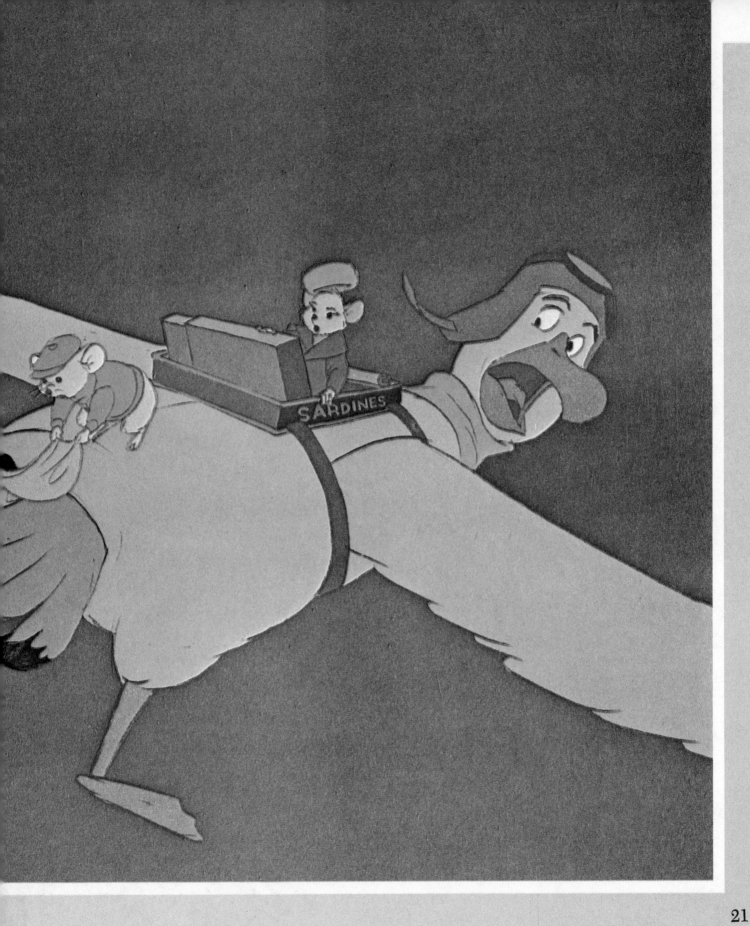

the porch of his tumbledown shack. He held a small jug in one hand, and he'd just taken a drink from it when the skyrockets went off. "My lands!" Luke exclaimed, staring at the flashing, whirling lights. "This new batch of swamp squeezings is the strongest I've ever tasted!" Then he called to his wife who was inside the house. "Ellie Mae! Come here!"

Ellie Mae was a round, happy-faced swamp rat, and she came out onto the porch just in time to see Orville dive toward the ground with his tail feathers on fire. The albatross crash-landed in the swamp and doused his smouldering feathers in the water. Then he blinked at Luke and Ellie Mae. "Flight Thirteen just made a perfect emergency landing!" Orville bragged to the two swamp rats. "Have you seen my passengers?"

"Here we are!" Bianca called as she and Bernard dropped from the sky. She was as calm and unruffled as usual. "My, that certainly was an exciting trip, Captain Orville!" she exclaimed. Then she looked at Bernard, who was greatly relieved and was stamping his feet as if to assure himself that he was on solid ground again. "Oh, Bernard!" Bianca giggled. "Your tail is frizzy again."

Orville introduced the two mice to Luke and Ellie Mae, and Luke very kindly offered Bernard the jug of swamp squeezings. "Have

a drink of this," he said. "It'll unfrizz your tail in a hurry."

Bernard took a drink. Not only did his tail unfrizz, but his eyes bulged out and his ears twitched and his whiskers twanged and he quickly decided that a single drink of Luke's swamp squeezings should last him a lifetime.

It was then that Bianca explained how she and Bernard had come to Devil's Bayou to find a little girl named Penny. "Penny?" Ellie Mae echoed. "That's the child Madame Medusa is keeping captive on the old riverboat."

Ellie Mae scowled and declared that she would like very much to give Medusa a few whacks with her rolling pin. And Luke took a big drink from his jug and declared that he and the other swamp folks would like to run Medusa out of the bayou. "What do you plan to do, Bernard?" Luke asked.

Before Bernard could answer, a frightening roar came from the swamp, and a blinding light stabbed through the darkness. It was Medusa in her Swamplaunch. Bernard and Bianca watched the spotlight sweep across the swamp and then stop when it found a small, blond girl cowering beneath a tree. The child held a teddy bear in her arms. "That must be Penny," Bianca said to Bernard. "Rufus the cat said she never went anywhere without her teddy bear."

Suddenly, two alligators slithered out of the shadows and crawled close to Penny. One of them took her teddy bear in his teeth. The other one nudged her almost gently. "Oh, I should have known you'd find me again," the mice heard the child say. "All right, Brutus,

23

I'll go back to the riverboat. Nero, don't you dare get my teddy bear wet!"

Penny trudged away, and Medusa's cruel laugh echoed across the swamp as she roared off in her launch. "Those alligators are Medusa's watchdogs," Ellie Mae told Bernard and Bianca. "Every time Penny tries to escape, Medusa sends them out to bring her back."

"That's terrible!" Bianca exclaimed. "We must follow them! We've got to help Penny!"

"You're going to need a boat," Luke said thoughtfully, and then he shouted into the darkness for someone named Evinrude to wake up, and for the first time Bernard and Bianca noticed that a dragonfly was sleeping on the stem of a large leaf floating in the

swamp near the cabin. The dragonfly woke with a start when he heard Luke call, and he held firmly to his leaf. His wings moved so rapidly that they became a blur. Buzzing like a motorboat, he propelled the leaf to the shore.

"Evinrude," Ellie Mae said to the dragonfly, "Bernard and Bianca want to follow those two alligators. You can take them across the swamp in your boat." Ellie Mae then wished the mice good luck as they got aboard the leaf-boat, and she told them to send Evinrude back if they needed help. Evinrude's wings buzzed again and the leaf began to move over the water. Soon they were racing in pursuit of Penny and the alligators. The two mice peered into the gloom, and Bianca gasped when she saw the child and the two great beasts disappear into a bank of fog that hung low on the surface of the swamp.

The dragonfly raced his motor even faster, and the leaf-boat shot into the blanket of white mist. "Slow down, Evinrude," warned Bernard. "We can't even see where *we* are, much less where Penny and the alligators are going."

Evinrude stopped his frantic buzzing and settled on the stem of the leaf, and for a few moments they drifted silently through the haze. Suddenly two huge shapes loomed up in front of them. It was Brutus and Nero. They were coming fast, and it was too late for Evinrude to steer the boat out of their way.

Luckily the monsters did not see Evinrude or the leaf or the two mice. Brutus swam past on one side, while Nero sped by on the other. Bernard gasped with relief. He thought they had escaped safely. But Bernard had forgotten that alligators have huge tails. Now Brutus' tail swept through the water toward the boat, churning up a great wave. That wave swept over the boat. Evinrude and Bernard were drenched, but Bianca was washed into the swamp! She vanished beneath

the surface for a second, then bobbed up again and cried, "Help! Bernard! Help!"

Bernard did not stop to think about his own safety. He held fast to the edge of the leaf with one hand and stretched as far as he could toward Bianca. For an instant he was afraid he couldn't reach her, but a second wave bounced her back toward him. He caught her hand and pulled her onto the boat. "Are you all right, Bianca?" Bernard asked.

"Of course!" Bianca was dripping, and she had been quite frightened, but she still could manage a little laugh. "I knew you would save me, Bernard!" she said.

Evinrude fluttered his wings then, and Bernard saw that the dragonfly was far from all right. With wet wings, Evinrude could barely move. He surely couldn't send the leaf-boat scudding over the water. "Evinrude, do your best," pleaded Bernard. The mouse reached over the edge of the leaf and began to paddle at the water with his hands. "I'll help," said Bernard. "We'll get to shore."

Working together, the mouse and the dragonfly managed to propel the boat out of the fog and up onto a sandbank, and there they saw Madame Medusa's riverboat. Bernard climbed off the leaf and helped Bianca ashore. Then, after asking Evinrude to wait in case he was needed, he and Bianca crept through the swamp grass, past the gangplank where Medusa's Swamplaunch rested. It was tilted at a crazy angle. Silently they climbed the anchor chain to the deck. Bernard pointed to a cabin window where light showed. They climbed to the window ledge and peered inside.

The large salon of the riverboat was furnished with worn-old chairs and dusty divans. The carpet on the floor was threadbare. The drapes had once been beautiful, but now they were faded and streaked with age. An ornate pipe organ stood against one wall, and the mice could see a wide stairway leading to an upper deck. They could also see Medusa pacing up and down the room. She was in a rage, and she carried a cane in one hand which she shook at Mr. Snoops. "You fool!" she shouted. "If Penny had escaped, my plan would have been ruined!"

Snoops whined and cringed and blamed the alligators, who sat in the corner watching. It was they who had let Penny get away, said Snoops, and it was he who had locked her in her room after they brought her back. "I know how to handle that child!" he declared proudly. "While you were off in New York, she brought plenty of treasure up from the cave!" Snoops dodged around Medusa and ran to a

desk on the far side of the room. It was piled with glittering jewels. "Look at all these gems!"

"But I want the Devil's Eye!" Medusa slashed with her cane at the jewels and they scattered over the floor. "This trash is worthless compared to the Devil's Eye. It's the most valuable diamond in the world! We know that Waldo the Kid and his pirates hid it in that cave. Penny is small enough to be lowered through that hole into the cave. Once we put her down there, there's no reason why she can't stay and hunt until she finds the Devil's Eye!"

"But she's afraid to stay down there very long," Snoops explained. "There's an underground opening to the ocean, and when the tide comes in, she's afraid." He took off his glasses and wiped them. "Also, she's afraid that her teddy bear will get wet, and she won't go anywhere without that teddy bear."

"Dear Snoops, you don't understand children." Medusa put the tip of her cane under Snoops' chin and smiled. It was a nasty smile. "You must gain their confidence. You must make them like you. If necessary, you *force* them to like you!" She swung the cane at Snoops, who ducked away just in time. "At the next low tide I'm going to put Penny down in the cave! I'll keep her there until she finds the Devil's Eye! Now I'm going to get some rest so I'll be ready, and I suggest you do the same." Medusa marched up the stairway to the deck above. After a moment, Snoops followed her. And no sooner had Snoops left than Bernard and Bianca crept in through the window and took shelter under a chest of drawers. "Bernard, that woman is insane!" whispered Bianca. "We must get Penny out of this dreadful place!"

Bernard completely agreed. Before he could think of any clever way to do this, however, he became aware that he and Bianca were in trouble—terrible trouble. Brutus and Nero had sniffed the perfume Bianca was wearing. They had followed the pleasant scent and now two ugly snouts were poked beneath the chest and two pairs of beady eyes blinked at Bernard and Bianca!

The mice ran for it! They skittered and scampered around the room, and the alligators came after them, snarling. "The pipe organ!" Bianca cried. "We can hide in the pipes!" Like a flash she leaped to the keyboard of the old pipe organ, and then jumped again, straight into one of the pipes. In a twinkling Bernard was also hidden in a pipe.

Brutus growled a low growl and crept to the keyboard of the organ, while Nero climbed above the organ and watched the

pipes. Furiously, Brutus began to slap at the organ keys with his paws, sending air whooshing and booming through the pipes, and sending first Bernard and then Bianca bouncing out of the pipes. As the mice flew up into the air, Nero tried to catch them. He missed. He missed again and again. They kept escaping back into the organ, while Brutus kept hammering at the keys and the noise shook the old riverboat. Then at last Brutus pressed exactly the right key and held it exactly long enough, and Nero was in exactly the right place. Bernard flew out and Nero caught the little mouse in his mouth.

But before Nero could swallow Bernard, Madame Medusa came racing down the stairs and rapped the alligator on the head with her cane. "Nero!" Medusa screamed. "How can I sleep while you and Brutus are making so much noise?" Crack! The cane came down

again. Nero's mouth popped open and Bernard tumbled out, and suddenly Madame Medusa forgot all about being angry—or sleeping. "A mouse!" Medusa cried. She jumped up on a chair and wailed in terror. "Help! Snoops! Help me, you fool!"

Snoops came running with a broom and he tried to hit Bernard. First he missed Bernard and hit Brutus. Then Bianca jumped out of the organ and Snoops tried to hit her. He missed and hit Medusa. Medusa shouted and Snoops banged about some more with his broom, pounding wildly at the floor wherever he thought a mouse might be. And while he pounded, Bernard and Bianca scooted up the great stairway to a long corridor which was lined with doors. From behind one of those doors came the sound of sobbing. It was a child crying. Bernard and Bianca had found Penny!

Penny did not think it at all strange to have a conversation with a pair of mice. The little girl wiped a tear from her eye and hugged her teddy bear when she saw Bernard and Bianca, and she wanted to know where they came from. They explained about the Rescue Aid Society, and about the way two agents had found the bottle with the note in it. They told about their visit to the orphanage and their conversation with Rufus the cat, and how they had come by Albatross Airlines to rescue Penny. And when Penny wondered aloud why they hadn't brought the police with them, Bianca gently pointed out that big people don't always listen to mice the way little people do.

Then the three of them began to plot. They had to get away, and quickly, but there were the alligators and there was Madame Medusa and her Swamplaunch. They decided at last that Bianca would use her perfume to lure Nero and Brutus into the old-fashioned cage-like elevator aboard the riverboat and that Penny would slam the doors on the monstrous watchdogs so that they couldn't pursue her through the swamp. Madame Medusa could be kept busy—very busy indeed—if they set off Mr. Snoops' supply of fireworks in her cabin, and they could use Medusa's very own Swamplaunch to flee.

"It's our only chance," said Bernard, "but I don't think we can do it all by ourselves." Without waiting for the others to comment, Bernard leaned out the window. "Evinrude!" he called to the dragonfly. "Go and tell Ellie Mae we need help! And hurry!" A moment later, Penny and the mice heard the buzzing of Evinrude's wings. The dragonfly was on his way, and no doubt Luke and Ellie Mae would soon be at the riverboat. But then Penny began to tremble. There were footsteps in the corridor—the angry, hurrying footsteps

of Madame Medusa. It was time for Penny to try again to find the diamond called the Devil's Eye, and the little girl knew that Medusa would take no excuses.

◆·◆·◆·◆·◆·◆·◆·◆

Bernard and Bianca rode in Penny's pocket while Medusa and Snoops took the child to the cave. When they reached the place, the mice understood why Medusa needed Penny. Only a child could get through the small shaft that led from the surface of the earth down into the cavern. "Teddy doesn't like that cave," Penny murmured, holding her teddy bear in her arms. "He's afraid."

"Ah, poor Teddy!" Medusa said mockingly. Then she snatched the doll away from Penny. "You get down there and find the Devil's Eye," she ordered, "or you'll never see your Teddy again!"

the sea water comes in," said Penny. "I'm afraid to go back there."

"Oh?" said Bernard. "Well, if I were a pirate, that's where I'd hide the Devil's Eye!" He squared his little shoulders and tried to

Penny had no choice. She got into the wooden bucket which Snoops had tied to one end of a long rope and was lowered into a fearful cavern where weird shadows darkened the walls and water dropped over moss-covered rocks. The mice leaped from her pocket as the bucket touched the sandy floor of the place. They stared about them at the pirate loot which had been left by the notorious brigand, Waldo the Kid. There was a tarnished sword stuck in the sand. Wooden crates were scattered about, and there was an old sea chest filled with small gems, strings of pearls, and golden goblets.

"I've already looked in that chest," Penny told Bianca and Bernard. "Medusa doesn't want those things. She wants the diamond called the Devil's Eye!" Penny stopped and listened. A deep, rumbling sound came from far back in the cavern. The noise grew louder and louder, then faded away. "That's where look extremely brave. "I'll go and check it out."

He left Penny and Bianca and went deeper into the cave. He found a huge hole in the floor. Gurgling sounds came from it. He couldn't see to the bottom of the pit, but as he stared into it the noise grow louder. Then a huge geyser of water shot up and drenched him and almost pulled him down into the hole. Bernard's tail frizzled. He was afraid.

He was very much afraid. But he had seen something. Beyond the frightful pit in the cavern floor, something gleamed.

"I've found it!" he called. "I've found the Devil's Eye!"

Penny and Bianca came running. They watched Bernard, frizzy tail and all, as the frightened mouse edged his way along a narrow ledge that stretched beside the pit. The sea came up again and again, but Bernard pressed on. Penny helped Bianca across the ledge. "Over here!" Bernard called from the shadows. "The diamond is stuck in these rocks!"

It was. The enormous, dazzling gem was locked between two great stones. The three of them worked together to pry the diamond loose, but it wouldn't move. And the roars from the pit were louder and louder. The geysers that shot up were higher and higher. The tide was coming in!

"What can we do?" Penny asked the mice. "We'll be drowned if we stay here. And if we don't get the Devil's Eye up to Medusa, she'll do something awful to my teddy bear!"

Bernard found the answer. There was a pirate cutlass hidden behind the rocks. Penny was big enough to use it. She could pry the diamond out of the place where it was wedged. And she did, as the pit roared and a wave of sea water poured into the cavern and swirled around them. The little girl seized the Devil's Eye in one hand and the two mice in the other. She fought her way back across the ledge and ran to the place where the bucket sat beneath the hole in the roof of the cave. "Pull me up!" she shouted. "I have the diamond. Pull me up!"

Snoops did pull Penny up, and Bianca and Bernard and the diamond. Medusa screamed with delight as the bucket came up through the shaft. When it reached the surface she snatched the jewel from Penny's hand. "At last, I have it! A perfect diamond! And the biggest one in the world! And it's mine! All mine!" She spun around and walked away

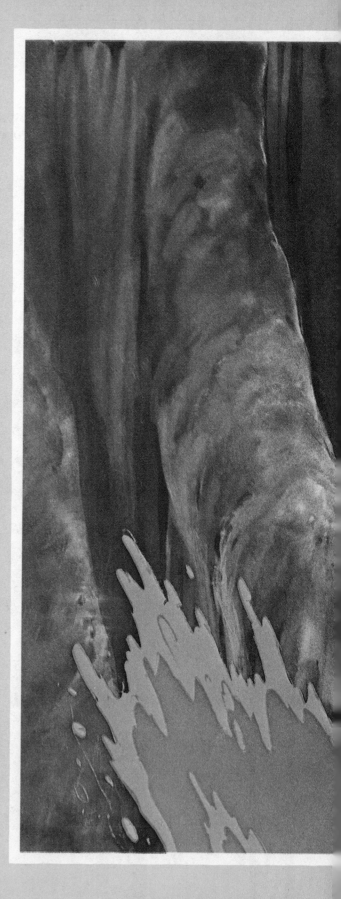

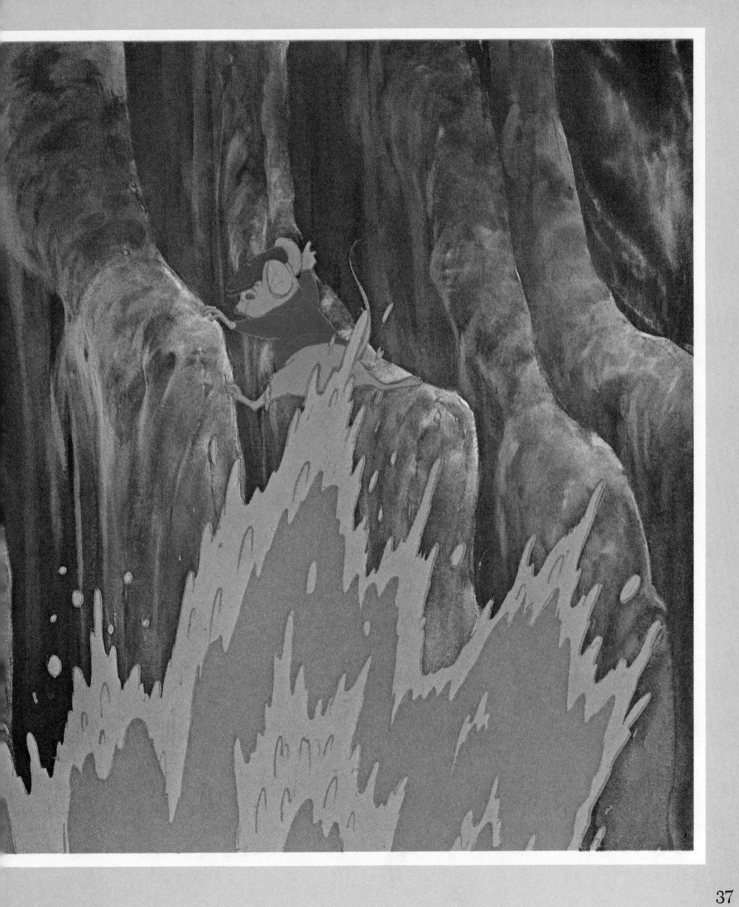

toward the riverboat. Snoops went after her protesting loudly. The diamond wasn't Medusa's—not all of it. It was half his. She only called him a stupid jailbird. And so, shouting at one another, the two wretched creatures went up the gangplank and disappeared into the riverboat.

"They're gone!" Penny said to Bianca and Bernard. "But Medusa took my teddy bear with her." Bernard was grateful that they had not taken Penny, and he was about to suggest that they all get as far away from Medusa and Snoops as possible. Then there was an ugly snarl from the shadows. It was Brutus and Nero. Bianca and Bernard scampered to hide in the tall swamp grass, but for Penny there was no place to hide. The two beasts slithered from the water and growled. Penny had no choice. She went back to the riverboat with the creatures.

Bianca felt that she might weep, but suddenly Luke and Ellie Mae came running up. With them were all the animals who lived in the bayou—Turtle and Owl and Mole and Rabbit—and one looked more grim and determined than the other. "Evinrude told us you need help," Ellie Mae said to Bernard and Bianca. "We're ready to save that child from Medusa!"

Bernard shook his head. "I'm afraid you're too late. "We haven't got a chance against those two alligators!"

"Yes, we do have a chance!" insisted Bianca. "Bernard, remember our plan? We lure the alligators into the elevator. They'll follow me there. They like my perfume. And we use the fireworks to keep Medusa busy."

It was their only chance. Bernard explained it to the others, and they all crept silently to the riverboat, sneaked up onto the deck, and peeked through the window into the salon. There was Medusa holding Penny's teddy bear in one arm while she waved a huge shotgun at Penny and Snoops! "Don't move!" Medusa warned. "If either of you tries to follow me, you get blasted!"

Snoops called Medusa a double-crosser and Penny begged for her teddy bear, but Medusa answered both of them with an evil laugh. "I have had it planned like this since the very beginning," she said. "And Teddy goes with me! I've become very much attached to him." She backed toward the door of the salon.

Owl and Rabbit quickly took their places, one on each side of the door. Rabbit, who was an avid fisherman, had brought his fishing pole with him, and he cast the line across to Owl. They pulled it taut, and Medusa tripped on it and fell on her back. The shotgun flew out of her hand and went off, blowing a large hole in the ceiling. She dropped the teddy bear.

"The diamond!" Snoops shouted. He pointed at the teddy bear. The seam in the back of the little stuffed animal was partly open, and the gem gleamed from inside Teddy. "The Devil's Eye!" cried Snoops. He dived for the teddy bear. Medusa had scrambled up, and she tried to seize the toy, too. There was a nasty thud as Medusa and Snoops bumped heads. The teddy bear skidded away from them and Penny picked it up and ran out onto the deck!

"My precious diamond!" Medusa howled. She grabbed her shotgun and ran after Penny, screaming for Brutus and Nero. Penny had a good head start on her, however, and as the little girl raced along the deck she almost stepped on Bianca. "Quick!" said Bianca. "Run for the Swamplaunch!"

Penny dashed into the shadows. Bianca looked back toward the salon. Nero and Brutus were coming in pursuit of Penny. Bianca laughed to herself and pulled out her tiny perfume bottle, which she always carried. She sprayed a bit of her enchanting scent into the air. The alligators stopped and sniffed, then forgot all about Penny. Bianca ran ahead of them, leading them back and forth and up and down and all over the riverboat until they were completely confused. At last Bianca

scampered to the old cage-like elevator, sprayed it with perfume, then ran on and hid. Nero and Brutus followed the scent right into the cage! Rabbit and Mole dashed out of the shadows and slammed the door shut on the alligators.

Just then there was a rumbling from outside. It was Penny, trying to start the Swamplaunch. "Penny's taking my Swamplaunch!" Medusa screamed from the upper deck, where she had been searching for the little girl. "She'll get away with the diamond!" Medusa ran to the railing and fired her shotgun at the launch. Pellets punctured the gas tank, and gasoline sprayed out in every direction. Penny leaped from behind the steering wheel of the

launch and jumped to the lower deck of the riverboat.

"Dear little Penny!" Snoops charged at the child. "Give me that blasted teddy bear!"

As usual, Snoops was clumsy. He snatched at the toy and Penny nimbly stepped out of his way. His rush carried him past the little girl, over the railing, and into the water below.

Down in the engine room of the riverboat, Rabbit, Owl, Mole, and Turtle had found Snoops' supply of fireworks. Rabbit held his trusty fishing rod ready. Owl lit a match and fastened it to the fish hook. Rabbit then made

a perfect cast, and hook, line, and match flew into the pile of fireworks. The match landed on a fuse which began to fizz and sputter, and the animals ran for their lives up the steps to the deck.

Kerrr-room! The first of the fireworks exploded. Then the rest began to go off in blazing fury. Several large skyrockets shot up the elevator shaft, hit the bottom of the elevator, and bounced it high into the air. The two alligators trapped inside the cage hung on in bewildered desperation. An instant later the elevator dropped back to the deck and smashed open. The stunned alligators discovered that they were free!

On the upper deck, Medusa was surrounded by bursting rockets, whizzing pinwheels of flame, and snapping firecrackers. She screamed and raged, and while she did so the little swamp animals jumped onto her launch and began to plug the holes made by the shotgun blast. They used whatever they could find. Rabbit used the handle of his fishing pole in one hole, and Luke even contributed the cork from his jug of swamp squeezings. Then, when they had every hole filled, Luke gallantly poured the swamp squeezings from the jug into the gas tank to replace the gasoline that had leaked out. "This'll burn even better than gasoline," he predicted. "Now we're ready to go!"

Ellie Mae called, "Penny! Bernard! Bianca! Climb aboard! We're ready to leave!"

Penny, Bianca, and Bernard jumped into the launch. Penny slipped behind the wheel and pressed the starter button. The engine wheezed and coughed, but before it would start Bernard shouted a warning. Penny looked up directly into the double barrels of Medusa's shotgun. Medusa took careful aim this time, and she would not have missed. But before the evil woman could pull the trigger, Owl flew in with a lighted firecracker held in each claw. Owl jammed the things into the barrels of the gun, where they exploded with a roar and split the barrels open.

Again Penny pressed the starter button. This time the engine on the launch came to life. But before Penny could shift the gears and get the craft away, Medusa leaped aboard from the riverboat. With a triumphant laugh, the woman grabbed for Penny. The little girl stepped down just as hard as she could on the gas pedal. The Swamplaunch shot forward. Medusa screamed, lost her balance, and tumbled over the side and into the water!

Unfortunately, there was a long rope trailing from the back of the launch. Medusa seized it and hung on. The boat moved faster and faster. Penny zigged and zagged and turned and veered, but Medusa clung to the rope like a grim water skier. She wouldn't give up!

And another danger lay ahead. Brutus and Nero had left the riverboat and were lying in wait in the swamp. As the launch sped toward them, they opened their huge jaws, ready to crush the craft with their teeth. Penny saw them just in time. She swerved, and when the alligators snapped their jaws shut they missed the boat and cut the tow line. With a last angry scream, Medusa sank into the water!

While Penny and her friends raced away through the bayou, Medusa swam back to her riverboat. When she climbed onto the deck, Brutus and Nero were already there. "You worthless fools!" screamed Medusa. "You walking handbags! You let Penny get away with the diamond!" She picked up her shotgun and whacked the brutes on their heads. "Take that!" she shouted, "And that! And that!"

It was too much even for Nero and Brutus. The alligators turned on Medusa. The evil woman dropped her ruined shotgun. She began to run. And when, from a safe distance, Penny looked back at the riverboat, she saw a final burst of skyrockets lighting the decks. And she saw Medusa clinging to one of the tall smokestacks.

"Poor Madame Medusa!" Penny said. "Now she knows what it's like to be a prisoner!"

"Don't worry," Bernard said. "Nero and Brutus will keep her there until you can send the police to get her."

"And *you* will have to send the police, Penny," Bianca pointed out. "The police aren't in the habit of listening to mice."

◆·◆·◆·◆·◆·◆·◆

Orville carried Bernard and Bianca back to New York on Albatross Airlines. When they arrived in the city, Orville ignored his usual landing strip and made his descent right in front of the United Nations Building so that Bianca and Bernard could make their report to the Rescue Aid Society without delay. The members of the Society were gathered in the Assembly Hall when Bernard and Bianca entered, and everyone shouted and applauded. "Welcome back!" the chairman called to the mice. "We've already heard what a fine job you did helping Penny!"

Bernard was surprised. How could they know so quickly? But then the chairman went on to explain. "Penny was on television. I doubt that anyone really believed her when she told them about talking mice and an albatross named Captain Orville and Evinrude the dragonfly and all the other creatures in the swamp!"

"Grown-ups never believe things like that," Bianca said with a sigh.

"Now don't be downhearted," said the chairman. "Penny is being adopted by a very nice family. And perhaps they understand more about animals than most grown-ups; they're adopting Rufus the cat, too!"

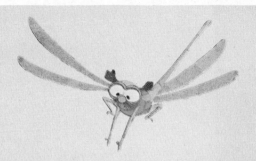

The chairman then announced that this meeting of the Rescue Aid Society was adjourned, and he ushered the foreign delegates from the hall. For a few moments, Bianca and Bernard were left alone. It was the end of their mission. It was time to say good-bye. Bernard looked down at himself and he felt gloomy indeed, even when Bianca assured him that he was a very good agent—and that he was extremely brave, even if his tail did frizzle at times.

"Bianca," Bernard said at last, "I'm going to miss you *very* much."

"My dear Bernard," whispered Bianca.

But then a familiar buzzing sound filled the room, and Evinrude the dragonfly darted in carrying a tiny note. The chairman hurried in as Evinrude, exhausted, coughed and wheezed like a decrepit outboard motor and settled to rest on a desk.

The chairman took the note from the dragonfly and he read it hastily. "I say, this is critical!" he exclaimed. He looked around the Assembly Hall. "I need a volunteer for a new rescue mission!"

But all the delegates to the International Rescue Aid Society had left—all, except Bianca and Bernard. The two little mice looked at each other, and both broke into huge smiles.

"Mr. Chairman!" Bianca and Bernard cried. "We volunteer!" Then, laughing happily, they hugged each other and set off together on another adventure.